I0575739

No Wonder

Poems

By Elizabeth G. Howard

Copyright © 2025 Elizabeth G. Howard

All rights reserved. This book, or part thereof, may not be reproduced in any form without the written permission from the publisher or author, except for the inclusion of brief passages in a review.

First Edition

Print ISBN: 979-8-9923691-0-6
e-ISBN: 979-8-9923691-1-3

Cover design by Elizabeth G. Howard
Edited by Jessica Klimesh
Set in Avenir and Garamond

Printed in the United States of America

dedication

mothers—
an as-yet undiscovered
species of succulent:

surviving
unfavorable periods
by dying back,
their bodies
swollen,
fleshy in
appearance

a well of juice,
ornamental,
cultivated for
hardiness, for
a striking
appearance, for

an ability
to thrive
on mere
mist and dew
fasting healing
equipped to
endure—

--

For my mom, who didn't understand but always loved me.

For Cathy, Frances, and Lane.

For my trusted partner, Colin.

Table of Contents

"The woman's body is the terrain
on which patriarchy is erected."
- Adrienne Rich

Section One

unsettled

everything's fine! i say
the cat rips up the junco
the sun glances away

on the road from home to home

outside
(beyond my bothersome brain)
the earth is so gracious.
once again,
on the road from
home to home,
i give myself over to
quiet consumption
of her perfect form,
this time in barren autumn
after the harvest
after the fall,
where fields give way
to the horizon,
where subtle curves
heave and gulp the road,
where clouds shift
in dollops and hordes
on the cool blue blanket above.
aniah and i gab
in one direction,
inflating the van
around us—
the other way,
dad is quiet,
counting cooper's hawks,
pointing out the deer family
frolicking on the corn-stubbed hill,
under a splashy sun.
every car passing:
another imperfect soul
gripping the wheel,
another portal
into an unknown heart.

number

i wish to be counted,
i wish to be whole.
i've been named
obtuse, irrational, negative—
as if i were
an imaginary number,
useful but not real.

there is no code for me,
no binary measurement:
only fractional
equanimity, unsolved
proof—one theory
rolling into the next
into abstraction.

people love sunrise

people love sunrise
but they also love sleep.
so they usually miss out
on the poured morning colors.
sunrise, a mute awakening.
the way night is banished
the way day remembers
who she really is.
sunrise occurs
for only an instant,
namely, the moment when
the sun's upper limb appears
tangent to the horizon.[1]
but also
astronomical dawn,
civil twilight,
smudged by atmospheric effects,
extend the painted breath
into protracted minutes
while birds serenade
while clouds decide
where and how
while hate snoozes its concerns
while babies doze—
so are we in our dream state.
a woman consumes the dawn.
how tender is the shrouded
heart, how harmless
the sleeping gun, how pure
the sun's bloody ray
pressing over
the soft shoulder
of a day.

---

[1]"What is the length of a sunrise?" from Wikipedia
<https://wikipedia.org/wiki/Sunrise>.

i reach out—often

with
a feather or a song,
or, once in a while,
a hammer.

i am always making of myself
something of what you are.
and sometimes you make yourself
something of me.

what is required?
maybe all that is
required is to be alive,
to breathe.

burnished

how the shine blinds
the effort. so little
record of the sweat
jettisoned in the rubdown.
below the stairs
so many backs
thrown into
the polishing
the scrubbing
muted soles
stifled grunts—
we prefer our
labors invisible
our lives to glow
facilely; let
no one know
how many
abortions
missteps
bungles and busts—
let me have been
born on a summit
on a summer's eve
wrapped in sublime mist
without a single
push or sloppy
placenta
without any
mother
to speak
of

the wrecked thing

angry people aren't all that popular.
when someone explodes,
the air empties of humanity:
souls vanish;
breathing's left
on hold while
the wrecked thing
    troubled,   still smoking
gathers its skirts and handbag,
somehow
and stumbles
out.
my oh my!
tornado of relief
as the door slams.
laughs wobble while
forms rematerialize,
solidifying in a watery union of
what the heck
was that all about?
someone passes 'round
judgment cookies.
feel free to dunk them
into amnesiac tea.

care

we strangled him, i guess you could say.
perhaps that's what he would say.
we read the ghost writing on the wall,
let our panicked hearts imagine
how it could play out, grasped harder,
turned up the volume of love, while he
jammed his fingers deeper into his ears,
trying to gouge out his brain.

it's a sorry, dry trickle
to unfamiliarity— you can't see it
in the holiday photos,
vacay videos. memories can be
desolate gaps, bloody gashes.
care sometimes comes with letting go—
that is to say: caring enough to not care:
tested for an hour, then a week.
after year or so, time forgets itself.
on days like today,
the scab flaps in the breeze.
lately, there's been too much acid hope.
have you ever sat down on a floor
cradling a tangle of christmas lights,
moving a bulb through rabbit holes of time?
inside those plastic cloaked vines, a harbinger;
one can't rush or the hair-thin conductors
snap, and that's the end of it. lights out.

still, i keep on trying to clear it all up,
as if everything is meant to find itself
back on the sensible straight line,
back on course for the great future.
it's just a mess, with
zero way to recycle it.
care learns to turn the face away:
find light from another source
than wishes and dreams
in candy colors.

disconnected

you won't realize
               how
dis con nec ted
                    you had to
       become
until you retell   the
                        story

       u
        n
          s
           p
            o
             o
              l
               i
                n
                  g

details
      once again
     but
this time
        it gushes out
                  in shrieks and
                        wails.

11

give me your body, your blood

let me know if there is
anything i can do
she commented dutifully
on the post, and
i thumbs it up. what
can be done by
vibration, other than
a reused prayer?
thoughts have
power but give me
your body, your blood,
your wholehearted presence
to change the atmosphere
to shove the storm clouds
aside. show up on
my doorstep unannounced
with warm baked goods—
wash the dishes,
hold me tender and hard.
this is no virtual crisis:
i am crumbling
before your eyes, should
you lay eyes upon me.
a wolf arrived some weeks
ago and tore me up, swallowed
my spirit, now marinating
in her gut, sliming through
her bowels—no. she isn't
visible to you but even so
i am dissolving—
what shape have i left?
i need you, your
body, your bones, your
flesh made visible
to persist,
to get upright
to maybe
live at all.

human

i'd like to have more options.
i'd like to break more rules.
i'd like to have more space, or
to be able to make use of the space i have,
differently.

i'd like to undo things,
sort the pieces out on the table
and take a look at them
as they are. maybe
this isn't the best
configuration.

maybe it's ok to let it all lie
in bits for a while, with
room beside
and among.
seems like there's space,
so why not take it?

i'd like to set a few things
down and leave them there—
see how they do.
see what happens to them
through the seasons,
through a night.
what happens to me
without. i have permission, but
i have ties, responsibilities,
agreements.

it's hard to be
human. nothing is simple,
yet everything is.
the earth turns,
the sun sets,
time passes, and
i choose things,
or not. i sleep sometimes,

or i don't. i eat.
things get quieter,
things get interrupted.

the dog sighs.
a train clatters, and drags on.
the barred owl asks its question.
seems like there's space to be had
so why not take it?

i conflate myself with expectations.
i conflate success with joy.
i conflate tomorrow with hope.
it's hard to be
human. things get
interrupted.

enough

today is the birthday of someone but who—
does it matter who is born?
one person breathes in and
one person exhales and that is
the sum total of life and death.
and because we are 100 percent
certain we are all there is,
that one life matters, one cell matters,
a passing is marked,
while the night sky, in its
infinite wisdom tries
(every. single. night.)
to shout to us
the truth: that
we are nothing.
it assembles the stars
in their order
again, though
billions of miles away
and already dead,
to tell us—
again—
you there, on that patch of
earth, crying in the
dark, laughing at aziz,
eating a funnel cake:
you are nothing and
that had better be
enough.

they know something

i've never been brave enough
to get a tattoo. it's not the
pain that concerns me—
it's the inscribed meaning
attached to ink symbols—
such brash permanency
promised to all who see,
on the tenderest organ.

what does it say?
they come closer—
but already without
knowing
they know something—
a woman able to
carve an idea
into the stone of her body
to shout, to spill.
even before she speaks
she's spoken.

my body is quiet.
should i carry
scripted affirmation
to ensure i am
enough? what does it say?
they come closer,
but no second glance.
this echoless parchment
requisite,
and yet.

Section Two

home

in this field of dreams—
hold down the shifting landscape
prop up the falling sky

i want my heart to grow even wider

i want my heart to grow even wider:
what's a metaphor that works?
not the deep canyon.
not the unknowable sea.
not the speckled night sky going
on and on into the infinite.

what's awake but not sleepy,
open but not naive?
what's warm but makes way
for a cooling breeze?
what's truthful and lean
and kind and sharp,
worthy and imperfect—
full, but with space:
willing but wanting?

what is a metaphor that
works, that takes it easy,
but refuses to give up?
what's that thing that
knows love is heartbreak
and that heartbreak is
life and that life is
this moment and that
this moment is
all i really have?

i want my heart to grow
even wider, but
i'm busy
doing living things, and
thinking i'm not
loving right and
second-guessing
which way to steer
into
the skid.

i remember being 14

there's a new middle school
on my daily walks
patchy grass smattered
with motivational signs:
an idea whose time has come
and gone but lingers while
raging parents ban books
vote in racist board members
pay at the altar of a cult church
vote for the orange shit gibbon.
every day a wave of poor sweet souls
pass through those doors,
last hopeful minutes
sliding away with them,
their pores wide open
absorbing maternal love and
gun panic in equal gulps.
i remember being 14,
life a swirling wonder,
trying to catch onto
what i needed to have
who I wished to be
while hiding from
the creep inside.
i did theatre then,
my weird freckled face
coated with greasepaint,
my coat hanger body:
the floppy scarecrow.
my cicada spirit:
the unoiled tinman.
my soul: the shivering lion.
i read *teen beat*
wanted shawn cassidy
modeled wonder woman
made note: how to protect
delicate skin under my eyes
improve my posture
my skin, my style

my total package.
I remember being 14
being myself
a framework for tomorrow
those last hopeful minutes
when there was still a chance.

fallow

i have been so seduced by bed of late.
i lay down flat and melt into it,
disappearing into the threads,
into the folds, into
cast-off dreams.

i am trying to remember when
i took the exit ramp, when
i left the whining highway,
rolled down onto the quiet
edge of unfurnished backroads.

i let this vehicle carry me out
into the fallow fields,
routes slicing through,
hip-hugging, repeating railcars
holding me in place.

i forget to use my mirrors.
now and then a feverish
f-150 tries to eat my tail.
it's a jolt to be discovered
out here, hounded, alone.

i pump myself full of
meadowlark cries,
cloud shadows,
moldering grass, and
twilight clasping the day's hand.

i have been so seduced
by resting, by far corners
of a parking lot,
by broken concrete,
gaps in time,
the fluids, leaking out.

at the hospital, with my dad

it snowed this morning
though no one predicted it.
the two baristas arrived
on time anyway,
to layer lattes and cold foams
in the caff in the lobby
behind the glass doors
inside the sterile building,
the marble walls pinging
with sighs and bells
of the elevators
carting family, lovers, and
nervous CNAs up up
and away.

i'm at the hospital,
with my dad, and it's ok—
he's ok. he's 85 and this
obstruction is minor,
a veer on a slippery road,
but we know now
how not to oversteer,
how to turn into the skid.
i arrive to relieve
my sisters, my brothers,
a rotating tag team
to hold space
to chase down
clear liquids,
to walk circles
with him in the hall.

nobody likes to be alone—
when does one stop planning
the next holiday,
the next road trip,
and simply wait for
the inevitable?
the PT on her rounds

marvels at dad's speed;
the OT gapes at his flexibility.
the lead-gray day
tricks the eye:
clouds' underglow bathing
his rowdy, unfinished
heart.

some babies are rhinos

do you ever wonder about
the dragon? her fire scorching
the hillside, burning everything
down—such deeds tossing her
dreams to nightmares, such
violence making her
cry herself to sleep?

what is my fault?
i wonder about this as
i let the cymbalta slide down.
what am i to blame for,
what may i lay to rest—
what outbursts and frenzies
erupt when my mind's
rubbed raw with discontentment,
curdled by its own
science experiment?

how many years should i walk
the tightrope of self-discovery?
one day forgiving myself
one day adorning myself
one day battering myself
one day hiding from myself
all the same.

some babies are born
rhinos. some babies are
born bunnies. some
snort and trumpet their wild way,
others are silent and
shivering under the deck boards.
when on the occasion of
growing up and older
we find ourselves, still,
tangled in night terrors
in soaked sheets
brain on the rack—

how do we find our way?

do you ever wonder
about the dragon?
her fire burning
everything,
crying herself
to sleep?

in the event

to all whom it may concern:
this is to let you know
i have taken hostage
your son, your husband,
your father. he went with me
quite willingly, with
no coercion. however,
he's asked that i tell you
he's quite captive and
cannot possibly escape.
he's asked that i tell you that
in order for him to survive
you must drop all his
favorite socks and
coffee beans and that one
pair of levis into a black duffle
and place it
under the park bench
at 12th and main.
in addition, could you please
include at least one pair
of comfortable shoes and
his passport.
you should know that
in the likely event
he does not return
visit www.allrightalready.life
for updates on his welfare
and whereabouts.
we hope you won't delay—
no one wants more than me
for your beloved to be
safe and sound and
to feel loved in
this time of uncertainty.
yours truly, thief of the heart.

last night i dreamed of you

last night i dreamed of you
again, as if you took yourself
out wandering and stumbled
into my reverie.
i knew it was only a wish, or
the overlap of two wishes:
one keening out over the miles
one harbored and eclipsed.

do you wonder if you matter to me?
you are with me
everywhere, every day.
i go on walks into the field
which rumi told about,[2]
hoping you'll find your way.

i lie down and wait.
moon rises and i drop
into dreams, you smiling,
jabbering, thank god, no more
wearing that mantle of fear.
i whisper back from shadows,
drinking in your every detail:
shirt wrinkles, nose shine
forearms roped in strength.

have you brought with you
the left-over foreboding?
i have forgotten nothing—
i know exactly what you worry—
i shove away despair's prodding,
as the sky pinkens.
dew, please stay!

---

[2]Refers to Rumi's poem "Out Beyond Ideas of Wrongdoing and
Rightdoing," translated from Persian in *The Essential Rumi* by Coleman
Barks.

hold us down!
lend us at least
one more moment.

voluminous

outside, evening comes by,
collects the falling day.
cicadas emerge from branch slits
the osage orange
the black walnut
a hidden symphonic ritual
on summer's shoulder,
unconcerned with
storm's shudder or
bloated heat.
voices crescendo then
stop without warning—
voluminous, filling
ether as spirits do
as frost does
as sakura may—
summer burdens me most:
its deep shadows,
its corpulent rains,
grass too green to gaze upon,
wobbly allium, coreopsis spread,
an ocean of ditch lilies—
my senses give up
as the day gives in
but still the tree crickets
drone on, though
maybe a bit
sleepier, slower.
air brings me woodsmoke
while girls laugh at intervals—
this is the blue i need—
twilight keeps it,
damp and ready
to give over to
night,
so roomy
so generous
so vast

say nothing at all

let no one refer to this
stately loblolly as
"plant." how long
the unswerving pine
has endeavored
to grow straight up
leaving hillside behind,
shedding needles,
dropping cones
losing parts when
the ozark storms
push her around.
how long has she
defied gravity,
coiling
taproot in
loamy sand,
sedate rocks,
silently drawing
hope from spring? no
hands put this
ancient one here—
she made her own way
resisting disease,
development, the
goring pests wanting
to control her insides.
leave off sound
to marvel
at her graceful arms
holding sky, holding
the citrus summer tanager
while she consumes
the sun.
call her a tree
if you must, but rather
say nothing at all.

what a mom is

a mom is god on this green earth,
the maker of people.
when a mom dies
maybe her soul goes to heaven
but she never leaves.
i know for certain
after 10 years passing,
her being always by my side.

a mom lies awake
years after her kids
move out, wondering
are they safe
did they eat
are they drinking water
did they change their oil

did i do enough?

a mom lets you down,
says wrong things—
slivers of cutting words
that etch into memory
in between the
tidal waves of
forgotten giving.

a mom eats last
sleeps least
worries most
forgets to
pack her own food
for the trip to the zoo.

a mom dies
trying
dies waiting
dies wishing

she'd done better
done more.

a mom holds
onto you
at every age
cutting and pasting
hot cross buns
hockey assists
homecoming dresses.

a mom creases
and folds and
wrinkles and
expands into
stretch waistbands
grasping at
love scattered
like dandelion
seeds.

again and again

you warn me: "i'm sweaty!"
"bring it" and we
pull each other in,
unmasked.
i drop my face into
the curve of your wet neck—
one by one
we fall together,
wringing each other out
again and again
the night through.
welcome to our happy
steam bath,
love pumping,
a/c heaving,
everybody schvitzing,
how the liquids flow.
prosciutto disintegrates;
mojitos fade away.
there'll never be another
good or better time for
goodbyes.

hold still

there's nothing here
that i can demand
to hold still

though try as i may
to ensnare it, to trick it,
to lure it into a bog.

i am born to die, and
here i am doing it,
spinning wild-eyed

through space,
using up the days
like cheap sparklers,

guzzling tomorrow
on hot wheels,
worrying the road.

there's no one here to
stop and stay. i'll use up
a parade of blue-black days.

Section Three

off, again

hometown—night calls out.
i take a walk, passing by
myself in shadow

just killed a man

i don't care.
every rocket is a phallus.
change my mind.

shot up into space for
reasons unintelligible,
we blow up boys.

i prefer silence.
even after the thunder,
let's bathe in the abeyance.

80 years, give or take
(mostly take, from what i've seen),
and this is your plan.

/any way the wind blows
doesn't really matter
to me.   mama/

you have to stop
look to see. there.
a wilderness. a space between.

rocks in a jar don't fill it.
rubble won't neither.
every rocket is a phallus.

i prefer silence—
change my mind.

it's always been

that same
old song
shivery pulse
twilight glow
tender air
though
now and then
i couldn't hear it
and sometimes
i tuned it out
forgetting years—
its name
its notes
beguile again
its smoky taste
underpinning
the november wind

a broken poem

i tried to write a broken poem
but my will resisted, my
heart said please don't do it!
stay here where it's safe,
on the downy cushions
on the level surfaces.

stay here, glued to ice—
do not unravel old ideas,
fossilized wishes, dreams laying
ass up in the gutter,
waiting for someone to
admire. stay still.

stay still, don't move
lest you tumble
into another acid
love song, into
another soggy wander,
into another blind chance.

this is not the time,
nor the age to
leap into blizzards, to
pull on your skates, to
scamper or hustle or
paint your dusty
whore. stay still.

don't move.
get yourself
together.
what good
ever came from
the dawn?

a muscle memory

i am drowning in my loneliness,
a simmering world over a smoky fire.

i gaze at the digital elephant
walking tail to trunk on a grassy plain,

my heart stumbles:
is this real life? am i alive?

i push myself out into space.
i make myself human again,

out into the electric noise
in the awkward stand of

white bodies swaying to
the knockoff Dead band—

it's hard to even locate
a muscle memory, we're all so

dehydrated of love.
i never was an introvert—

but now it's a defense mechanism
used to block out the humming

meanness underneath,
the house of humanity

slides away in the flood,
incinerated in the fire.

the terror, the wonder
of daily truth or dare:

what lies beneath the façade
of this smiling stranger?

no wonder

no wonder i wish you back with me.
days come i lie
on the hammock in the shade,
letting moments sink into each other
until i disappear into them.
it's one thing which remains the same:
memory. i am gone now
to cairo, having jostled my way
across an 8-lane roundabout
wild with car horns hot
rubber flapping burqas
and the sharp stone crawling
into my sandal, calling up to me
remember! a moment of now
embedded into tomorrow—
such postcards i would never
send. no wonder i am
heavy: i worry whether
i'll ever be seen.
i've stood in front of
a starry night, in front of
cattle in touraine
two-dimensional dreamscapes
better telling the story of
me than this face ever could.
what a poor vessel is the body
to carry undulating stories
so precious and so ready to
be spilled. no wonder i find myself
morose at being looked upon
as if this façade were
the sum of it—
no wonder i sleep fretfully
inside windy dreams,
a speck grasping at
meaning while
the universe, herself,
rages.

the art of not beating myself up

it's a fine balance to
excuse oneself of one's
daily failings while
simultaneously keeping
inherent laziness in check.

somewhere along the
spectrum between
perfectionism and total
sloth-dom, i rise
to today's occasion of
to-dos.

on the one hand, i know i am
failing utterly at
living in the now
as i *check check*
check myself for the
ticks of timeline inadequacies.

on the other hand, work is
a measured pour—
no possibility of
getting plastered on its
feedback loop— or
of falling in love.

it takes time,
in sprints and naps,
unplanned days and
long swallows
to move forward and
to also
stay still.

my heart is settled
(ode to Cheech)

my heart is settled
even if i am not:
it knows as much as
the wind knows,
which is everything,
enough, and
nothing at all.
today, on The Moth,
Cheech Marin told
his story[3], and he was
quite adamant: call him
by any name, but not
Chong. he escaped
war by working clay
in Canada and then again
by breaking a leg
in half, he emphasized,
on a black diamond at
Whistler. what does
the heart know?
everything,
he seemed to convey.
it's where the ancestors
take root, come calling:
where you been, man?
my heart latched onto
his voice unspooling
as i drove across
our languid town,

---

[3]Reference to "The Artful Dodger," a story that aired on The Moth Radio
Hour in 2019. To listen to the 17-minute story, follow: bit.ly/cheech-
poem

acres for sale, zoned R-2,
red-tailed hawks
laying on the wind,
a water tower
waiting at a stoplight
because i missed the turn:
"in a quarter of a mile, turn left."
GPS Daniel prods me;
i pay no attention to
the road. Cheech puffs his joint,
stands in his undies
before the draft board,
brown skin, hair tufting
at his butt crack,
receding hairline.
the reluctant father
arrives in the story
with his to-do list.
and says to his son:
how's it going?
how's work?
and the heart cracks a little
and mends a little.
two men—
now both men—
laugh,
and the story ends.
my heart is settled
even if i am not.
it knows as much as
the wind knows.

advice to my younger self

girl, you do not have to answer every question.
you do not have to solve every problem.
you do not have to finish what you start.
you do not have to go all the way, anywhere.
you can keep the old model.
you do not need to upgrade.
you can leave your hair as is.
you can go without—
without makeup
without sleep
without reason or
means.
you can talk too loud and you can
be a little mean.
you will find yourself regretting
less than you think.
when you're tired, you don't have to keep going
though sometimes a two-minute break
will keep you going on just fine
and you'll be glad you did.
you can change—
change your mind
change your style
change your attitude
change your direction
change your viewpoint
you can forgive, but you don't have to.
you've got everything you need, and
plenty that others wouldn't mind sharing.
now and then, your dreams are going to
try to kill you, break you wide open—
the nighttime ones, and
the ones you've been dragging around
since you were five.
monsters need friends too.
don't forget to read a book
now and then—lay back on your pillow
like you used to do, all summer long
when you weren't this comfortable in your body

and let the story carry you away.
now and then be sure to
leave the house,
to spend time with someone
who says things you don't expect
who smiles at you in that certain way
who dances with their eyes closed
who pitches their tent outside reality.
now and then leave the house
turn up the music
and sing—because
singing is for the singer
and for the song—
and for no one else.

a good look

because spring masquerades with us
because friends continue to report
i can't breathe
because though my heart sags
daffodils dare to have their way.

because spring upholds its wretched promise
because friends scramble to apologize
if i'd only known
because sorrow remembers my shape
regardless of my shrinking trousers.

fill the holes, the advice calls.
Plug up all the places the animals enter.
from my window i scan the field of boards
count gaps like grains of rice
and the garden and the compost buffet.

mulch the beds. feed the sparrows.
stain the deck. hose the siding.
wash the storms. fix the wood rot.
while fullback yuccas lean into
the foundation and shrug.

because spring arrives regardless
because friends ask artlessly
what are you going to do
while anxiety strolls in with
attachments and homework folders.

i stop the walk for a long look—
perennials know something i do not.
can't you keep me forever
in this sweetness?
i touch the downy cheek and
the petal falls.
the dog drags on.

seedling

not much
to you—
three bits:
root shoot leaves.
so much
potential
though
you got no self-awareness
you can do
nothing but
shiver
suckle
stretch
yourself out
of a name:
such is
the nature of
every damn thing.

the imperative tense

keep walking.
keep looking
and taking a pic.
keep collecting beautiful things.
keep breathing through your nose.
keep texting others,
day or night,
saying i love you.
keep hugging and kissing.
keep reading books and
making handwritten lists
of those you love and who love you,
and birds, and flowers, and shrubs.
keep watercolors ready
out on the counter.
keep moving around
and stretch.
keep stroking and brushing
the pets (yours and others'),
and talking to the neighbor kids.
keep swinging on swings.
keep dropping off into naps.
keep the sink and the dishes clean.
keep making plans,
then show up
to dance, to look at art,
to jump on a bed, eat pizza and fart.
keep willing and upright and ready.
keep singing right out loud—
in showers and garages
and airports, in streets
on bluffs and also in bars.
keep leaving the house even though
you don't want to
to get milk,
to hear music,
to heal.
remember to take
a good look around

at the wind in the trees
and the roots reaching down:
this world still belongs to you.

live among the stars

the alarm jangles at 6:47 a.m. and
i slap it shut, dull morning datum
fingering its way into nodes.
i've left you again,
abandoned on the other side
to meander the cosmos.

you'll wait while i
dip bread into egg batter
while i stuff lunch boxes while
i fill calendars and execute
conference calls. you'll wait,
a once-blank canvas behind
scrawls of sharpie ideas and
frenetic spray paint:
such is a day.

you live among the stars,
swinging hand over hand
from ursa minor to
cassiopeia, waiting for me to
exit the scoundrel hours,
to leap upward into
your arms into the
possible into

the forgiving night.

ephemeral

what in this life is lasting?
we are but transient beings
pasting ephemera
onto a passing day.

what in this life is worth holding?
i wander the history books,
the thrift stores, draw hearts
in the dust, the cast-off skin.

nothing about me feels temporary
and yet the evidence piles up—
the flashing of the bird's wing
as it rushes to or from its prey.

my mind stretches out long tentacles
into eternity. my soul untethered to
any fences, my heart unbound, rejecting
definition, yet here i am so limited.

how thin are the pages of the sacred book,
the onionskin letters the soldier
mailed home, stored faithfully
in her attic all these years.

these years, compressed into reflection—
how many can one jam into the mirror's frame,
into the scrapbook's binding yet
memory unspools into terabytes?

i am waiting for something to happen
while one makeshift episode slides by after
another into neverland—
nothing about me feels temporary.

Acknowledgements

The poem "disconnected" first appeared in Issue 1 of the *Waffle Fried Literary Magazine*. Thanks to editors Kelsey Coletta and Benjamin Branchaud for publishing it.

Gratitude to Jessica Klimesh, who meticulously edited each poem and the collection as a whole. She is a great editor and an even better friend! If you find a mistake, it happened after she handed this back to me!

Gratitude to writers/editors Amanda Roth, Mary Sauer, and Frances Story of Salt Tooth Press. Three poems originally appeared in the 2023 anthology, *Stellification*.

My continued thanks to the Writers' Colony at Dairy Hollow for providing a beautiful residency space in Eureka Springs, Arkansas, for writers like me, and for introducing us naturally lone creatures to each other.

Many first drafts of these pieces first appeared on my Substack, *The Zed Review*. My sincerest gratitude to my "subscribers" and to the many who have read my work online these many years. Your attention, time, and support mean more than you know.

All my love and hugs to my kids and husband for being my sweetest cheerleaders. And so much love to my writing family, those worthy creatives and artists in Connecticut, London, Kansas City – and online! – who keep pushing me onward.

No Wonder
Poems

Elizabeth G. Howard is an
interdisciplinary writer who uses
poetry, video, and storytelling to
address gender, power, and
identity in the natural world. She's
published nationally and
internationally, including in *Boston
Literary Magazine*, *American Craft*,
eMerge, and *Bentlily*.

She is a Writers' Colony at Dairy Hollow resident, a Mid-
American Arts Alliance Artists Leadership Fellow, and Artists
Inc. Fellow. She writes Demand Poetry at live events on her
Olivetti typewriter. She lives in Lee's Summit, Missouri with
her family.

www.ingramcontent.com/pod-product-compliance
Lightning Source LLC
Chambersburg PA
CBHW050501110726
47899CB00003B/1035